Through The Third Eye

Aden Carter

Joan McHugh

Paperback ISBN: 978-1-7367416-0-3
eBook ISBN:

DEDICATION

This book is dedicated to 2020, COVID-19, and lockdowns for keeping us all inside and forcing us to find new means of entertainment.

CONTENTS

ACKNOWLEDGMENTS

We would like to thank those who gave us a chance, picked up our book, and gave it a good read. We hope you all enjoyed it and enjoy whatever it is we write in the future.

We would also like to thank Shyanne Carter of ShysArtStudio for creating the cover art of our first book. More of her pieces can be found on ShysArtStudio.com.

ACKNOWLEDGMENTS

Judgement

"My name is Amelia Wilson, and I have committed a crime, a sin, and an atrocity to my employer, Mr. Bill Morgan. I will be damned if they charge me any differently from my white coworker, a terrible and unholy woman who breaks the law for fun. I did my best to help my family through our hard times. My husband lost his job, my children were sick, and I asked the Lord to provide me a way to help us through. It was through my lack of acceptance and irrational thinking that caused my crime; Deborah should admit the same!" Amelia's words resonated across the crowd gathered in front of the Fulton County Courthouse.

News coverage exploded about the black woman who stole from a billionaire while working for him as a caretaker. *Wrongfully Sentenced,* headlines read, but it didn't help anything. Protestors lined the streets where Amelia's body was found two days after her sentencing. Courtland Avenue was home to attacks against police officers who started the violence.

It started on June 28th, 2020. Amelia awaited her trial, her husband teary eyed and her children shaken to the core with the idea their mother would go to prison. She was an upstanding woman after all. Never did a bad thing in her life, and her husband knew that.

Amelia headed down to Dee's Market on Edgewood in her trusty 2001 Crown Victoria, as she always did on Sundays. Silver paint reflected various buildings she passed; the sun's light reflecting and catching her eye at each when she stopped at a traffic light.

The media had gotten ahold of her story. Some rallied in her favor, others condemned her, but none of them recognized the role her coworker played in the matter. She spoke up about many of the wrong ideas people threw out about her and gave multiple speeches in hopes the truth would come out, but only a few crowds listened.

While driving to the store that beautiful Sunday, Amelia was pulled over. Busted taillight, but we've all seen just how far even a busted taillight can escalate. A seasoned cop stopped her who'd not only seen action but had also been the cause of most of it. He was one of those "bad apples" you read about in the news.

Nobody caught a glimpse of how it started, but it didn't take long before Amelia's body was on the ground, her back riddled with four bullets. The cop, as it so often happens, was never charged with the murder of Amelia Wilson.

Calls of qualified immunity rang out. Protests surged and rallied across the streets of downtown Atlanta calling for the sentencing of the cop who wrongfully ended the life of a promising mother over one small act of indecency. A taillight that would ignite yet another movement burned into the delicate peach skin of the chief of police and all of Atlanta.

You see, Amelia Wilson was a strong woman, independent and intelligent. She knew how to do the right thing and would never give in to false statements about her race or culture.

"Don't let anyone dictate who you are!" Amelia's mother preached to her when she was a little girl growing up in Lakewood Heights. From a young age, Amelia listened to her mother go on and on about being a stand-up member of the community in which she lived.

Let's take a look back and you be the judge of Amelia Wilson.

Talk of police brutality flew from porch to porch in Lakewood Heights. Amelia grew up with fear of the police instilled in ger heart, along with the hearts and minds of her neighbors, most law-abiding citizens.

Amelia worked hard to get out of the ghetto. Each day, word of new struggles from cops raiding homes to misunderstood situations ending in violence for unnecessary reasons and the governmental assistance promised but never delivered threatened to take away the soul of the 'hood,' but Amelia powered through on the words that echoed from her mother's vocal cords.

She studied to be an RN at Herzing University and graduated top of her class. During her time there, she met a man who boosted her spirit and kept her grounded. Alex Wilson another American in his prime with a chip on his shoulder from acts of racism from a young age.

The two of them were inseparable and soon after graduation purchased a home near Rawson-Washington Park, away from the crime and fear of Lakewood Heights. It wasn't long before they brought two children into the world, both with kind eyes and laughter that could make even the saddest human being smile

Alex took up a job working for the police. He wanted to give back to the community and bring the change he hoped could help close the racist gap that plagued the city. It was that very mission that ended his career when he was forced to step down after admitting problems in the system.

This left Amelia as the only one employed in the house with two children barely old enough to walk, but she made enough to support the family. She found a job working for wealthy man in the city who lived off Durant Place in a beautiful two-story modern home.

The job was easy, Amelia had to clean Bill's house, remind him to take his medication, help out around the house, cook meals, and run a few simple errands. She was happy working for him, and he was happy to have her company. It wasn't until Deborah Hannity started working for Bill too that things took a turn.

Deborah was a hateful woman. She was one of

those women whose picture of the perfect life was a man taking care of her every need despite being a strong, independent woman herself. She had her moral values and hated anyone who tried to go against her way of thinking, most likely stemmed from her upbringing.

Her father was a Christian man. Strong willed, devoted, and always the provider, despite hardships. He was a man who genuinely believed that above all else, God should be everywhere. I guess you couldn't blame Deborah for turning out the way she did. She was handed everything to her as a child, despite not being the brightest nor the most honest person.

It is an amazing thing that trust funds offer kids. When Deborah's father struck it rich from the stock market, he decided to quit work and pursue life living the way other rich men lived. Deborah had everything she could want as a child, thanks to dear old dad. And also, thanks to that, she never knew what it was like to work for anything.

If she needed a car it was, "Daddy, I need a car." If she wanted a new wardrobe it was, "Daddy, I want new clothes." He always delivered, knowing he would have wanted his parents to do the same. Which is why it came as a shock to Deborah when she moved out and daddy expected her to get a job and stop mooching off the family's wealth.

Her father set up a trust fund with advisors, just in case she failed or anything. In fact, it was her trust fund that bought her house, funded her college career, and bought her a brand-new Lexus, but there was never a thank you or even a nod of appreciation. It was always take, take, take.

While Deborah was at Herzing University, she came face to face with inequality but always felt the need to side with oppressors. She always found it fun, and when confronted, would claim she wasn't racist.

She later found the man she chose to marry. Surprisingly to her friends, he was a strong, hard-working man. Devoted, just like her father. Neither of them saw any problems with the world and continued their heavenly experience like nothing wrong ever happened. And nothing wrong ever did happen. Not to them.

Deborah's husband had a cushy job making eighty thousand a year, but they still used her trust fund for a stipend each month claiming his salary wasn't enough for them to live on. Privilege in its finest, but they were ignorant to everything about it.

They lived in the upper middle-class luxury for years. They went on vacation, bought unnecessary things, and threw money away like scraps of paper. It wasn't until spring 2019 that they finally felt the burden of their ventures. With the economy weakening, Deborah's husband lost the job he thought was secured with a tight connection with his boss. Deborah pleaded with their trust, but they had finally had enough and wouldn't increase her stipend. She was forced to get a job.

Now, this may seem like such a petty thing to complain about. After all, a job is something that most people have. Most people travel to their place of employment, do their work, and make it home in time to do it again the next day. A never-ending cycle humans are forced to participate in day after day.

Deborah used her connections with other wealthy friends to land the same job Amelia had. Easy enough to do, but too much for Deborah to handle.

"You can get that, right?" Amelia heard a thousand times throughout the day. But her favorite thing was when Deborah would say, "I can't do it, I just got my nails done." Amelia knew it wasn't true, though. Deborah had her nails done every other week but acted as if they were done each new day.

Amelia and Deborah often fought one another over the chores, Amelia always losing or giving in to do them anyway.

"Keep your head up and don't let anyone push you around," Amelia's mother's voice rang in her head every time, but she never listened.

"I'm being the bigger person," she always told herself.

It wasn't until the second week of July that Amelia discovered Deborah had been stealing items one by one from Mr. Morgan's home. They were small items, excess coins that looked valuable, diamonds left unattended, and silverware custom made for Mr. Morgan's wife.

Amelia thought to bring it up to Mr. Morgan, but ultimately thought that Deborah's recklessness would end up getting her caught. Amelia didn't want to cause trouble despite her distaste for Deborah.

Times were getting harder for Amelia's family, and

she knew Deborah felt the effects of a failing economy as well. Deborah's normal high-end lifestyle was cut off, and she had to do something to keep herself in the high life.

"Why do you keep stealing stuff?" Amelia finally got up the courage to ask as she scrubbed the lavish bathroom on the second floor, far from where Mr. Morgan could hear. Deborah stood nearby cutting her nails with a gold laminated set of nail cutters.

"What? Me? I haven't been stealing anything," Deborah replied with a slight gasp. She wouldn't ever get used to accusations, true or not. In typical fashion, her hand fluttered on her chest in rich-girl dramatics as she faked surprise.

"Yes, you have. I saw you take one of Mrs. Morgan's necklaces the other day. It was the piece Mr. Morgan bought her for their fiftieth anniversary."

"You better take that back, or I will report you!"

"Take it easy," Amelia spat back at her. She tossed down the rag she was using on the toilet and stared Deborah down with fierce eyes only a mother understands how to use.

Deborah stepped back and stood within the doorway to the bathroom. She took a deep breath with closed eyes. "Okay."

"So, I will ask again. Why do you keep stealing from Mr. Morgan? Are you not getting paid enough?"

Deborah walked out into the living area that

connected to the bathroom. She dropped back into the couch with a large sigh. "No, I am paid quite nicely. Likely more than you."

Amelia followed her, calmer now, and sat on the marble block fashioned into an ornate coffee table. "Then what is it? Do you get a rush out of it?"

Deborah bent forward, placing her elbows to her knees. "A little… But it's more than that. You ever get a chance to experience the finer things in life?"

"Can't say that I have."

"Well, when you get it, there is this overwhelming sense of urgency to keep and maintain that lifestyle. Public appearances, self-grooming, and above all else proper, having the money to back up your words. Without any of that, people who once showed the utmost respect, just disappear. Friends, family, the lot of them."

"So, what your saying is, you need to maintain public appearance of being wealthy or you're afraid everyone will eventually leave you?"

Deborah nodded.

Amelia chuckled. "Well, ain't that just the craziest thing I've ever heard coming from your mouth."

Deborah sprang to her feet, nostrils flared. "It's not crazy! It's the truth. You just wouldn't know, being from the ghetto and all."

Amelia took a deep breath with a long, exaggerated

exhale. "You're right. I don't know what it's like, but could you at least try working a bit harder? Doing all this excess work is making my back hurt."

Deborah whipped her hair to the side with her hand. "If it means I won't have to deal with you getting on my ass, then sure, I guess I can do a few more things around here."

A new streak began. Deborah was more helpful. She continued to steal, but the constant thought of looking over her shoulder made her more cautious, more paranoid. Amelia wasn't one to blackmail people, but it helped motivate Deborah, so it was worth it.

Months rolled on, winter brought snow and hardships. Bill Morgan became sick and, bedridden. Amelia and Deborah were more needed than ever.

Mr. Morgan's home had one section that remained under lock and key with a brown mahogany door, intricately carved with strange symbols, that stood as a guardian. Bill would often enter the section of the house by himself, and whenever Amelia or Deborah questioned him about it, he often alluded to something else.

Amelia, the more trusted of the two women, was tasked with cleaning it after Bill called her to his bedroom where he handed her a brass key with two prongs that stuck out of the end in opposite directions.

Amelia anxiously crossed the dark hallway to the large door. No windows provided light, just a dim, slightly worn-out chandelier with crystal hanging on thin wires.

She stuck the key into the lock. "What are you doing?" Deborah sprang forth from behind Amelia.

"Nothing. Just doing my job," Amelia replied. "Just go away."

"Is that any way to talk to a coworker?" Deborah tried to get her hand on the doorknob, eager to enter before Amelia could.

Amelia quickly removed the key. "I said, get lost."

Deborah put her hands up, "Hey, don't shoot right? I'm just having a little fun."

Amelia scoffed. "Get out of here before I tell Bill about your little habit."

Deborah gave up. She marched away, head held high, her typical entitled attitude.

Amelia waited for Deborah to disappear before turning back to the intricately carved door. She placed the key in the lock once more and turned it. The lock creaked, the mechanisms spun inside, and a loud clank came from within the center of the wood.

The door squeaked open as a thin beam of light from the doorway widened, then dissipated quickly, revealing little in the room. Amelia reached for a light switch.

The light flickered on. Like no other room in the rest of the house, this one struck Amelia. The walls were grey, floor solid wood, and the paintings dark, all of bloody children, hounds, and forests. In the center was a pedestal with a glass top. A lone card sat inside, the tarot card of judgement, decorated with a ghoulish design of a judge covered in blood and golden edges.

Amelia reached for the card but found her hand shaking. The room, the effect it had, was like witnessing torture for the first time. Gruesome but not harmful. She grabbed her duster and went to work. By the time she was done, she felt a deep need for consoling, but all she had was Deborah.

Deborah waited outside the room, occasionally trying to convince Amelia to let her in. When Amelia left, she quickly locked the door behind her and stormed passed Deborah as though she were nothing more than an invisible force, easily moved.

"What the hell?" Deborah called out. She stormed after Amelia looking for answers, but Amelia was gone.

A car engine turned over outside. Deborah ran to the window and watched Amelia drive off with a distanced stare.

At home, Amelia told her husband everything she had seen in the cold, dark room. Together they pondered. What did the paintings mean? An omen of ill fate? A telling of enslavement? Amelia's mind raced with the possibilities while her husband held her close.

"It'll be all right," he said, clutching her closer. With the clock striking ten, they laid in bed ridding their bodies and minds of the much of the day, but Amelia could only stare at the ceiling and imagine those paintings.

Each painting told a dark story. Children drenched in blood, tortured, their hearts begging for escape. Release coming when they were set free, trailing blood behind them as they ran through the woods only to be hunted down like animals. Arrows pierced their skin leaving cuts and puncture wounds. The more blood, the easier to find, the quicker to death. Forced to flee, the children jumped off a rocky shore and plummeted to the sea below only to meet their maker on spikes of stone.

The scene played out like a movie in Amelia's head, complete with bad reel skips and burn marks. Her heartbeat pounded along with the film, keeping rhythm with the events that transpired. Slow in the beginning, by the end, her heat thumped so loud it could be heard through floorboards.

She thought of that insidious card covered in blood and gold. The wealthy elite's call to judgement that they would never receive. It sat in a case, mocking the very foundation on which it stood. The glass forever a symbol that justice couldn't reach them.

Something had to be done.

After a night of no sleep, Amelia's eyes were dark. She marched into the home of her employer to see Deborah laid out on the couch.

"Move," Amelia said, brash, all care had been lost. Deborah quickly scooched over with eyes full of worry.

"What's up your ass today?"

Amelia stared at the painting on the wall.

Silent. Images of the child play across the walls.

"Well, what is it?" Deborah snapped her fingers in front of Amelia's eyes.

Amelia blinked back into existence. "N…Nothing."

"Don't give me that shit. What did you see in that room?" Deborah grabbed Amelia's arm, but Amelia ripped it away.

"Nothing! Get out of here and do your work!" Amelia snapped.

Deborah wasn't used to being spoken to in that manner. She stood, her mouth agape staring at Amelia, who'd had the audacity to attack her multiple times during work. She raised her hand, but quickly lowered it and walked away.

Amelia continued to stare at the movie that played out on the wall of the living room in front of her. The expensive Peter Max painting played into the scene as a background piece, a small bit of salvation in the twisted fantasy that unfolded before Amelia's eyes. The painting cut through deep sorrow with its bright imagery.

By the end of the day, Amelia had done nothing. Her body stale as an empty husk, her eyes twitched in horror until Deborah snapped her fingers.

14

"Good job doing nothing, you lazy bum," Deborah said, her voice tired, face unamused.

"What did you say to me?" Amelia stood up fast, her hands in fists.

Deborah stood her ground, unafraid to get physical if necessary. "You did nothing all day! I worked my ass off!"

Amelia got closer; her eyes trained on Deborah like a sniper seeking their next target. "Like I don't do that on a normal basis? The nerve you have!"

Deborah hesitated. Terror filled her body, but she suppressed it momentarily with adrenaline. "I do my fair share!"

"Yeah and reap the benefits of theft!"

"I don't have to explain myself to you!" Deborah yelled, her voice fierce and her body ready to strike. "Back down before I put you in your place!"

Before Amelia could think, she lashed out and struck Deborah down who collapsed to the carpeted floor. "Still gonna put me in my place, White Privilege?" Amelia's breath was heavy, her eyes filled with rage. She raised her arm high again.

Then nothing.

While Deborah lay on the ground, arms up in defense, Amelia's arm fell back to her side. The images of the paintings returned. Deborah was nothing more than another child shrouded in blood, stolen and stricken down.

15

Amelia fell to her knees, anger gone, eyes sully with guilty tears falling to her jeans.

Deborah lowered her guard. Amelia's tears filled her regret. She slid across the floor and leaned herself up against the rose-colored couch. She placed her arm on Amelia's back. "Are you alright?"

"The children…"

"What children?"

"In the room."

"What did you see in the room, Amelia?"

"Children on the wall, blood on their palms."

"You need to show me what you saw." Deborah helped Amelia to her feet and placed her arm around Deborah like a soldier carrying a wounded partner from the battlefield.

Amelia stared as they approached the door, the hallway a long tunnel to the horrors that lie beyond. Amelia's hand shook as she tried to place the key in the lock. The key dropped to the floor. She clenched her hand. Her breath shallow, almost unnoticeable, her eyes wide as a deer's in headlights, she trembled.

Deborah grabbed the key and with a swift turn, opened the door. Cool air from inside wafted out into the hall.

The women entered the room. Deborah scanned

the walls.

Nothing. The paintings were gone, but the memories lingered like the cool air. Deborah let Amelia go.

Amelia dropped to her knees, her body weak. Tears flowed from her eyes and dripped to the floor.

"Is the card still here?" Amelia muttered.

"What? You mean this?" Deborah pointed to the judgement card that still laid in its glass casing. "It's just a dusty old card."

Amelia wiped her eyes, her makeup smearing across her cheeks. She darted to the case and there it was, the card, in all its bloody golden magnificence. "Doesn't it cry out to you?"

Deborah studied the card with Amelia, her gaze deep, breath held. Deborah stole a few glances at Amelia before sighing. "No, it doesn't."

"But how?" Amelia cried out.

"Maybe because it's just a card," Deborah said. She placed her hands on Amelia's shoulders. "Are you sure you don't need help? I'll prove it to you."

Deborah lifted the glass case off its pedestal and placed it gingerly on the carpet below. With a quick swipe of her hand, she held the card. "See? Nothing special."

She tossed the card aside like an unwanted birthday card. It fell before a large built-in bookcase. Amelia chased after it, desperate to hold it, but when she bent down to pick it up she noticed something strange.

A small button, just big enough to see under the middle shelf of the bookcase. Not in an obvious place, it could have easily been missed, but not clever enough that a good sleuth or sideways minded caretaker wouldn't uncover its whereabouts.

Her impulses guided her to push like a small child who can't resist grabbing a piece of candy instead of a healthy snack.

Click.

Amelia sat back with red eyes staring at the bookshelf as it opened. It felt like a scene in a movie or a book she liked. A treasure hunter finally found that missing piece, but for her, it wasn't anything precious.

No.

Instead, the bookshelf opened to reveal a small storage area, approximately 10' x 10' and it housed her worst nightmares.

The paintings.

The gory mess of caricatures were enough to make Amelia jump backwards on the ground. She pushed herself back as fast as she could until her back was against the pedestal, stalling her movements, but despite being blocked, she continuously flailed her arms and legs to keep her momentum.

"See! See! I told you they were real!" Amelia cried. She pointed to the evidence. "They're staring at me!"

Deborah stood dumbstruck; her eyes fixated on the crying children as they barreled through the woods. She could hear the cracking of branches, the howling of dogs, and worse, the drips of blood running from their small, pale wrists. Her impulses told her to look away.

She couldn't.

No. More than that. She wouldn't. Deborah felt the need to witness the story in full. She walked into the storage room, picked each painting up one by one and placed them in the order of the story.

Amelia watched in horror as Deborah did this, continuously trying to move back, but blocked by that damn pedestal and too wild minded to move around it.

Once Deborah was done, she fell to her knees. Before her was the story of many children, lost to those with power.

"Girls!" Mr. Morgan cried out from his bedroom.

"Girls! Could one of you come here please?" he called again.

Deborah snapped to. She quickly jumped over to Amelia and covered her eyes.

"Bill needs us. You go. I'll clean up this mess."

Amelia nodded with Deborah's hands still on her

face. "Lead me out of here, please."

The two women stood up and walked out of the room, all the while not uncovering Amelia's eyes until the paintings were out of view.

"Get yourself cleaned up, then go see what Bill needs. Got it?"

Amelia nodded.

"We'll discuss what to do later. Now, go!"

Amelia ran off.

Deborah reentered the Devil's chamber, the cool air welcoming her into her fresh hell. She quickly collected the paintings and laid them delicately back into the storage room without a sound. She left the bookshelf open and the door unlocked as she left and took her place back on the couch as if nothing had happened.

Just like Amelia, Deborah couldn't stop playing out the story in her head.

Amelia returned with the same blank stare and tired eyes. She placed her hand on Deborah's shoulder.

Deborah didn't flinch.

"We need to do something about those paintings," Amelia whispered.

Deborah nodded in approval. "But what?"

"We steal them. Tonight. Then burn them."

"Agreed."

The women tried to go about the rest of their day as normally as they could, but no matter how hard they tried, they couldn't escape the images that flashed through their minds. They made passing glances at one another to confirm their plans were still set, and as the day drew to a close, they wished Mr. Morgan a good night.

They stopped at the bottom of the long stairway outside.

"We meet back here in one hour," Deborah said.

"Are you sure he will be asleep by then?" Amelia asked.

Deborah pulled out a small bottle of sleeping pills. "May have added a little something to his nightly tea."

Amelia's eyes widened. "You drug-"

Deborah covered Amelia's mouth. "Shhh. Don't yell it."

"You drugged him?" Amelia whispered.

"Yes. He should be out any minute now. The door and bookshelf are open. We are all set."

They each nodded and went their separate ways.

Amelia used the time to call her husband. Her nerves spiked as the phone rang. *What will I tell him, I need to rob my boss?* she thought.

21

"Hey, Darling!" Alex said.

"Hey, Honey, I…" Amelia paused. She couldn't bare the thought of telling her husband about everything.

"What? What's going on?"

"Nothing… I might be late coming home. Accident happened. You know, bad drivers."

"Alright. Just be safe out there and keep me updated. I don't want to hear that my wife got into an accident as well."

"I will." Amelia clutched her phone like it was her final lifeline. "I love you, Alex."

"I love you too, Baby. Now, hurry up and get home. Your kids miss you."

"I'll try." Amelia lowered her phone. Tears ran down her cheeks.

She walked around the city for a while to clear her mind, but no matter where she looked, all she could picture were the children. She saw them on billboards, buildings, and busses. She saw them in the puddles on the street and the faces of strangers as they passed. She checked her phone, 9:45 P.M.

At 10 P.M. the women met up. Deborah had a corndog, a fun meal to remind herself of better times. She also carried a sheet under her arm.

"Grabbed this to cover them up."

"Good thinking. I… Is what we are doing wrong?"

Deborah took the last bite of her breaded treat. "No. Think of it as purging a demon. A sick and twisted demon."

"Okay…" Amelia said.

"Let's go." Deborah began walking up the stairs, her handing shaking as she gripped the railing.

They opened the door slowly, the alarm system turned off, nothing to worry about. The door to the study was to the left, not far from the main entrance, but as short as the distance was, it felt like miles to them. They crept down the hallway leaving the main door wide open for the cool air to waft its way in.

In their minds, the hallway twisted; the door melted away. It now resembled the gates of hell, their passageway paved in sin.

They opened the door, careful to lift it as to prevent any creaking, but the gates to hell are steel and bone; they will creak anyway.

"You might want to check if Bill is still sleeping. I'll wrap up the paintings," Deborah whispered.

Amelia nodded and turned around. She crept along the entranceway and up the twisting stairs to the master bedroom where Mr. Morgan lay. She peered through the cracked door.

Still asleep. Teacup still on his nightstand.

Amelia returned to Deborah who already had the paintings wrapped.

"Good job. Now let's get them out of here."

As Amelia bent down to help lift she noticed the card in the case had gone missing.

"Where's the card," she asked.

"Oh, this card?" Deborah joked as she held it between two fingers upside down.

"Why are we taking that?"

"It looked valuable. We may as well get something out of this as well."

Amelia scoffed. "Fine. Let's just get these out of here."

The women hauled the paintings outside and down the staircase. They were in such a hurry they left the door open and didn't realize that Amelia's jacket ripped on the iron fencing.

They threw the paintings in the trunk of Deborah's car, a large Cadillac Escalade, her favorite type of vehicle due to the amount of power it made her feel when she drove it.

Off they sped to the Silver Comet Trail, a bike path. Deborah parked on the side of the road, and they hauled the paintings a few miles into a tunnel secluded them from the rest of the world. It was there that they burned away their demons. It was there that the pain of the children in their minds were set free.

As they watched the flames, the movie in their minds played once more. The children bound and chased, beaten and enslaved, finally set free. It was as though the children waved goodbye even though the women knew they weren't really there. Their souls were brought to peace. Finally.

They watched the fire for hours. Each crackle, each ember, was another child freed. The story was broken, and if that was true, they got the judgement they deserved.

It was past midnight before the fire was nothing more than embers pooled in a pile in the darkened tunnel, and it was time for Amelia to return home. Deborah brought Amelia back to Mr. Morgan's home to retrieve her car. It was then that they noticed the door was left open.

Amelia ran up to the door as Deborah drove off. She quickly slammed the door and ran down to her car.

By the time she returned home, Alex and the kids lay sound asleep. Amelia took her place beside her beloved and contemplated whether what she had done was right.

Morning brought new life. The rising sun beat done upon the Earth. Amelia awoke with a fresh new breath of air that illuminated her body, relaxed her, and brought positivity. She welcomed her kids running through the house, a sight she hadn't seen for some time. She brought in the new day with pancakes, a meal she hadn't made for over a year. Instead, she left her husband to cook, but in this morning, Alex held her close as she stood over the stove.

A loud knock echoed through the house. Alex went for the door.

"Open up!" A voice called from outside. Harsh. The sound of sandpaper.

Alex opened the door to the sight of armed officers. His hands shot up into the air. Instinct. "Don't shoot," he called.

"We are looking for your wife. Is she home?" An old-fashioned looking man ask. His mustache screamed western movie. His beard, long and bushy.

"Honey?" Alex called. "The police are here."

Amelia stepped out from the kitchen with plate in hand but dropped it at the sight of four armed officers standing in her doorway.

"Kids! Run upstairs," she said as she walked up to the officers, ignoring the shattered plate on the hardwood floor. "What can I do for you, officers?"

The police officer in the lead towered over her. "Turn around! You are under arrest!"

Amelia, shaking at those words, turned around and placed her hands behind her back. "Please don't hurt me," she said softly.

The officer pushed her to her knees, a loud thump resounded as her knees hit the floor.

"Don't hurt my wife!" Alex said.

Ready for the backlash, the other officers pulled their weapons. "Back off!" they yelled. "Don't make us shoot!"

"It's okay," Amelia said as the officer slapped the handcuffs on.

"What is this about, Sweetie?" Alex said.

"Sir, your wife stole paintings from her employer. He called us last night. We have it all on tape." The officer yanked Amelia to her feet and shoved her out the door.

"Keep the kids safe!" she yelled from the sidewalk before being forced into a squad car.

Amelia was soon down at the police station in an interrogation room and cuffed to a table. The dark, expressionless room destroyed all hope from earlier moments like a vacuum. Amelia sat in tears and no amount of good thoughts could turn that around. Why had the children brought her pain?

She freed them, didn't she?

It didn't take long for lawyers to get involved. The case of Amelia exploded into a political nightmare, and Deborah was nowhere to be seen.

Deborah fled that night, off to a place unknown to many.

Amelia was left alone. She tried telling everyone

about Deborah, but nobody would listen. The case ignited protests. They called for justice because no charges were filed against Amelia's white counterpart.

Lawyers wanted Amelia to keep playing the race card, keep hamming it up for the crowds of people, and even though Amelia was caught on camera, the judges felt the sting of systemic racism crawling down their necks.

While some people rallied for her protection, some rallied against her. Others tried to dig up any information they could consider righteous.

Amelia couldn't help but to get swept up in everything. Her name was known all over the world and political parties. Talk shows and magazines wanted the story. The press helped her come up with it. She stole to help her impoverished family gain some semblance of wealth. Nobody even cared about the paintings. Nobody even asked.

The only time she brought up the paintings ended in disaster. Mr. Morgan had resources. The kind of resources that made it so that those horrible, life altering, mind-bending paintings didn't exist.

So, Amelia stuck to the racial story of the injustices that occurred. She spoke out. She called out Deborah, but she never came.

The trial commenced. Video surveillance was shown, but it only indicted Amelia. Deborah failed to be seen once again. It was as though she were a ghost, a figment of Amelia's mind. No. She had felt her, talked with her, argued with her. She knew Deborah was real.

The jury of her peers, six white men, five white women, and one lone black man, sentenced her to thirty years. No doubt influenced by the money of the wealthy trying hard to appease political members.

The fateful night came when she was killed. Nobody knew what happened. It was swept under the rug by the police. Amelia's story was famous. The cops knew that. The cop who stopped her knew it. After all, he was the one who locked her up to begin with.

He pulled her over for a busted taillight, but instead of a ticket, he billed her with her blood in the streets. He pulled her from the car, knocked her down, and put four bullets in her back.

Private investigations commenced. Alex didn't want to let it go. They fired the cop but paid him severance. The protests grew. They called for the cop to be put in jail. He was never tried. They never cared.

The protests lasted for months, but nothing good came out of it. Qualified immunity at its best.

When the snow fell once more, and it was clear that the issue had subsided, Deborah finally emerged. She stood over the spot Amelia was shot. Candles lined the sidewalk, flickering in the cold. Deborah opened her fur-lined jacket and pulled out the card of judgement, always upside down. Always ignoring the call to act, but that was her style.

The privileged never change.

The card fell away from Deborah's hand and landed on the spot where blood stained the road.

She walked away as Mr. Morgan picked up the card.

The Justice of Lovers

The air was thick and stagnant. Jase and his girlfriend Amber cut through the haze down an abandoned street, which was lit by a single flickering street lamp. She held on tight to Jase as they passed an alley way riddled with the regrets of the newly displaced. A red and blue sign glowed in the distance. It flashed on and off with the word "psychic, "accept the letters 'I' and 'C' were not lit. It was the only other light along the street that breathed life into the abandoned city. Jase leaned towards Amber and whispers softly into her tattooed ear with his British accent,

"Reckon they would have directions to the 'Fantastic rockin' coaster camp?"

Amber dug her elbow deep into Jase's ribs. Her skin was like soft cream against his caramel curves.

"Ouch! I was kiddin', geeze," he laughed. "But seriously, I haven't a clue where we are, love."

"As if a half-assed psychic could lead us in the right direction," Amber said.

"What, you scared?" Jase said as he playfully shoved Amber off of him.

"Not scared, I just don't give into scam artists who think they know me more than I already know myself."

"Well, we'll see about that, now won't we."

The couple stands outside the shabby storefront. The door is locked, but a doorbell is positioned above the door handle. There is a sign which reads: "Please respect the owners wishes and clear your mind. Enter with only good intentions, as you will be rewarded in your future despite your past or present indiscretions.

"For fucks sake," Jake scoffs. He bangs on the door.

A middle-aged woman approaches the door. She is covered in gold jewelry and wears a red long-sleeved velvet dress. Her eyes glare at Jase, and reluctantly she opens the door.

"There is a sign," she says in a low monotonous tone.

Jase shoves his way past the woman. "Yeah, well, signs are meant to be ignored, innit?

Amber and Jase stand in awe of the room. The room smells of burnt sage, and there are crystals showcased atop a shelf near a bookcase with books on astrology, palmistry, and tarot. At the end of the hallway is a curtain leading to another room. The couple make their way down the hall and pass the curtain. It leads them to a dark reading room. There is a table with a crystal ball in the center and a stack of cards positioned next to the ball.

"It isn't by chance you've made your way to see me," the woman says. "I believe fate brought you here."

"No, you are the only person open and we need directions," says Amber, "no offense." she cowers.

The woman sits down at her reading table and gestures Jase and Amber to sit. "Whatever you are looking for, I promise this was a part of your destiny. Come, sit."

Jase glances to Amber, who taps her feet in annoyance. She rolls her eyes toward Jase and gestures for him to sit first. She always looks to him for guidance, like the time in Santa Monica where she ran another car off the road. She claimed it was an accident, and Jase drove straight to her as the agent of diplomacy. The driver dropped charges and Amber was never found guilty of her obvious impairment.

Jase has always looked after Amber. It's how he was raised. His mother always said,

"A woman is fragile, like glass, but once you stare into the smooth surface long enough you will see your true self."

Jase knew exactly who he was with her, but often wondered if she made him this way. So, as many times

33

before, Jase took the first step and sat down on the velvet cushioned chair. The crimson fibers united with his skin, and formed a bond inviting a notion to let his guard down.

"So, madam, what could have possibly led me to your erm… shop?" said Jase.

The woman smirked. Her eyes toughened and the harsh reflection of the crimson velvet filled her eyes. "Come girl, sit. I'm not going to hurt you."

Amber reluctantly walks over to the woman's table, and sits next to Jase. Worry fills her eyes, as she does not know what to expect. She has always watched idly by while things happen to the people around her.

The psychic woman extends her hands, and draws in spirit energy to guide her through the reading. Her arms are adorned with bangles that jingle a soft tune along her arm. The gems from her long earrings gleam from the overhead light which bounces from her crystal ball, set perfectly in the center of table. Her eyes roll in the back of her head, and her lashes flutter.

"Pfft," Jase softly whispers under his breath.

The psychic juts open one eye, and glares at Jase with her eye glazed over with white.

Jase jolts back squeamishly. His fixates over her appearance.

"Ostende mihi viam," the psychic chants. Her hands guide her to the deck of tarot cards placed on the table. She lays them before Jase, still in a trance.

"In posterum revelare," the psychic chants. She flips over the cards and stammers at what they reveal. She stares at the reverse card of justice. She lays down one last card— the reverse lovers. The psychic gasps and looks at Jase. He smiles nervously.

"What?" he asks.

"You are to be married," she says.

Amber looks to Jase with a glimmer in her eye. She smiles wide, squeals, and squeezes Jase's arm

"I never said it was to you dear," the psychic says.

"Great fortune is upon you, but be cautious," she says. The psychic points to the reverse card of justice. "everything hangs in the balance. Your love life, finances, even your life depends on your next move."

Jase applauds her performance. He scoots the chair from under him and brings Amber to her feet.

"What a performance, bravo!" he says, "we really must be going now."

"What way is the festival?" Amber asks?

"One mile. Take a left down Denver Avenue, and you can't miss it," says the psychic.

"Great, come along Amber," says Jase, "let's get out of this freakshow."

They hurry out of the store front shop and scurry along the street. The psychic runs behind them shouting.

35

"You forgot to take your tarot card."

Amber shrugs her shoulders and retrieves it. She examines the card flipping it back and forth, and she smirks.

"Justice will be done. It's like a fortune cookie."

Jase shoves it in his pocket. "Right, let's get on with it then. Festival here we come."

Tires squeal in the distance. The sound of a modified engine comes barreling down the street. Amber looks behind her and in that same instance everything turns dark. The sound of Jase screaming echoes around her.

"No, Amber!" Jase cries out. He Wraps his arms around her and lifts her lifeless body up from the street, and looks onward to the car speeding away. Her arm is flattened and blood spools out from her mouth.

"Help me. Someone, please," he cries. He catches a glimpse of the psychic shop and wonders if it was actual fate that led him there. *What if we never entered. It's all in the timeline,* he thought. An ambulance approaches the scene. Jase still holds Amber, unable to let her go. The medical team insists on taking her into the ambulance. Jase breaks down and cries.

The hospital was gloomy from the flickering of florescent overhead lamps. The lights buzzed down the empty hallway and cast a shadow which illuminated Jase. He slumped in a hard-plastic waiting room chair. It was connected to others by a metal bar. Jase fixated on how lonely he felt in the empty emergency hall. The chairs needed to be filled with life, but all he saw that night was loneliness, and tragedy. *Could this be my future? Alone, surrounded by terrible lighting in hospital.*

The doctor approached Jase. Jase's heart sunk into his stomach. He could barely breath. *She's dead,* he thought. He stood up, waiting for the worst news of his life. A tear fell down his cheek and landed on the cold tile.

"It wasn't easy, and she fought as hard as she could. I'm sorry, but she's won't be able to walk again."

"Wait. She's going to be okay?"

"She's strong, that one."

Jase pulled himself together and wiped away his tears. "Can I see her?"

He entered Amber's dark hospital room. Monitors beeped as he walked to her bed. He placed his hand on her leg and his eyes watered.

"I love you." Jase whispered.

The monitors beeped once more. The sound rapidly increased as Amber's chest began to convulse.

"Nurse!" Jase screams. He whimpered and frantically peeked into the hall waving over a nurse. He buckles over and weeps. Snot drops from his nose. It's a horrific sound that Jase is belting out, but grief isn't silent.

Years roll by Jase. He is full into depression. Beer

bottles surround him, and he lies down on his single bed. Jase stares at the ceiling imagining his last day with Amber. This time in his daydream, they go to the coaster camp. They walk up to the flashing lights, and run through the park drunk on adrenaline. Then, Jase snaps back to what is really happening. He is consumed by sadness and disappears from everything he once knew.

Years pass, and Jase appears to be unrecognizable. A strong steel gate separates an estate from the street. Initials are engraved in the partition of the gate with the letters, "J" and "S." A long winding driveway leads up to the seven-bedroom, six bath pool house looking over a cliff facing the ocean. Inside looks like a spread of a home furnishing magazine with modern décor, black and white themed furniture and abstract paintings hung on the walls.

In the living room Jase sits on the couch looking out to the water. He looks older, like the pain of time has brought wisdom to his forehead. His confident nonchalant manner is replaced by responsibility, and worry. A woman in a silk robe walks toward him. Her skin glows in the sunlight peeking in from the window. She runs her fingers through his hair, but Jase does not notice. His mind is on the ocean in front of him. Jase focuses on each wave that crashes. As each one passes another thought is avoided.

"Babe, where are you?" she asks.

Jase snaps out of his trance. "Not now. Sidney," he says to her.

She tosses her long silky hair across her shoulder and leans closer to Jase.

"That's no way to treat your queen."

She grips his thigh, and squeezes as hard as she can.

"Now pay attention, lover boy," she says as she sits down on top of him. "I'm not leaving this spot until I have your undivided attention."

Jase sighs. He glances up at Sidney. "What?"

"I've noticed you've been in a sort of funk lately, and I will not have you moping around my house. It's bad enough I have to pick up your slack at the office, but now you're making me nurture you too? Give me a break." Sidney gets up and draws a long dark curtain over the window.

"You're right, I'm sorry. I should be happy because I'm with you, and you, Sid, are the only thing I will ever need in my life," Jase says.

"And don't forget I'm the only reason you're here right now," Sid says. She walks over to the bar and pours Jase a whiskey, neat.

"Yeah, about that," Jase interjects. "I've been thinking about maybe going into medicine. I think I've finally pinpointed the exact location in the brain where it switches off during a traumatic event. This could help millions who experience a comatose state. Amber ...I mean the last patient to experience long term trauma spent 17 years in a coma with brain regeneration. I truly think her case proves it is conscious, and it's able to repair itself through memory therapy."

Sid laughs. "You hear yourself? The only thing that matters is us." She rubs her stomach.

Jase stands up from his chair and walks over to Sid. "The only thing that matters?" he yells.

"I've spent my life working on stupid spreadsheets and listening to bullshit from the executives about market trends. That is what you are about. Me, the only reason I exist is to pull Amber out of her living hell."

"You seriously think that bitch can think? She's a vegetable, Jase." Sid wings her arm in the air with protest.

"She's withering away in some hospital bed on the tenth floor. I am right in front of you, full bodied, and bearing your child. I ruined my body for you!"

Jase clenches an ice pick. "Don't push me."

Sid sips on the drink.

"You're out of control," says Jase.

He snatches the drink out of Sid's hand. She pushes him away. In this moment Jase's pupils dilate, and an animalistic rage overcomes him. He cranks his hand back, holding the ice pick, and time slows down. Sid screams out, her face is frozen on the word *no.* Jase loses awareness of time as he is stuck in the frozen void. Before he knows it, his hand makes contact with Sid's stomach. Blood drains from her body and drips down Jase's arm. The blood sprays over his face after he removes the ice pick. This image does not stop Jase. He goes for one more blow. His face wriggles with each blow. Blood splatters all over his mouth, and behind him over the window, and the crystal glasses at the bar.

Images of Amber's helpless in the middle of the road flood Jase's mind. He finally comes too, and shutters at the lifeless body of Sid.

"What did I do?" he cries. He shovels the blood with his hands hoping to put it back into Sid's stomach. It drenches her clothes. "The baby! Oh, God. What have I become?"

Jase runs to the kitchen for cleaning supplies. He opens a drawer, where he discovers the card of justice. He looks at it, tilting his head sideways in confusion. The card is dripping with blood. He runs over to Sid and sloppily cleans up the blood. There really is no help with the mess. Each wipe spreads the crimson liquid into the cracks of the hardwood. The blood reflects flashes of blue then red. Jase stares at the pool, while his arms are forced behind his back.

Echoes of policemen surround the house, but Jase focuses his stare at the blood. He his pulled from the ground, and time resumes at normal speed.

The scene of the hospital is gloomy. It's a dark room with continuous beeping, but this time the beeping turns to an alarm. A dark figure sits up and pulls out the medical equipment.

Jase wakes up from a terrible dream. His room is dark, and all he can see is the reflection of the toilet which stands three feet from his face. He sits up, and looks over to the barred cell he now calls home. A sliver of sunlight peaks through the concrete corridor. A buzz echoes through the facility as they call for breakfast. Jase lays back in his bunk and covers his face with a blanket as rough as sandpaper.

Footsteps approach followed by a repetitive clanking. The steps frown nearer and stop in front of Jase's cell.

"Get up," a guard demands.

"I'm not hungry," says Jase. He rolls over in his bed.

"I never said this was a food matter, now get up. Put on a clean shirt while you're at it"

The guard escorts Jase to the visitor area.

"What's this? I don't *have* visitors."

"You do now, son."

Jase approaches a table where a woman and a child are sitting. He sits down and studies the person before him. She has long red hair, and scars along the side of her cheek. The other half of her face is covered by strands of hair, but he can tell it is disfigured by scar tissue.

"Do I know you?"

"You did in a past life," the woman says.

"Who is this?"

"This is my daughter, Justice. This is your daughter

too."

Jase chuckles. "Listen lady, I don't know who you are, but I sure as shit don't have a kid. Ask anyone in here." Jase rotates his body around the room. "In case you didn't already know, I killed my wife, and only chance at a kid. So, if we're done here, I think I'll just see myself out.

The woman brushes the hair from her face. A tattoo on her ear catches the attention of Jase.

"A—Amber?" he hesitates. Oh my god. How can this be?

She looks down at the table with shame. "They said a man who experienced an incredible loss dedicated his life to prevent such tragedy. When I asked the doctors what they meant, or who this person was, I never for once thought it would be you."

"I don't understand" says Jase.

"Your work. The police found it at the crime scene. I guess one of those idiots had enough sense to understand a breakthrough when they saw it," Amber says.

"I'm in shock. I can't believe it's actually you in front of me," says Jase. "Can you ever forgive me?"

"That's why I've come here."

Jase smiles and reaches his hand towards Amber, but she pulls back.

"You see, when I heard that a man murdered his

pregnant wife, I was sick to my stomach. I figured, why not celebrate the beginning of my new life, by bringing in another. So, here we are."

Amber displays her baby to Jase.

"Yeah, sweetie. This is the asshole who killed your mother," she whispers to the child in a baby voice. Her eyes piece into Jase's.

His heartrate increases and sweat drips from his forehead. He turns pale as if he's seen a ghost.

"Meet your 'not dead' daughter. Her name is Justice."

Murdering Anton

Jeremy Cricket was not the most colorful crayon in the box, in fact, some of his old classmates would call him an idiot behind his back. How could they not? He claimed to be a writer but could not produce a single original idea. He became the laughingstock of his graduating class.

Still, he tried each day. He would sit at his laptop, open his programs, and type away hoping that something good would come out of it. The most that would come out was incoherent garbage he quickly deleted.

He wandered the streets of Portland, a creative city, looking for inspiration that would take him to the next level. Something, anything, that screamed, "I need to be written about!" Nothing caught his eye though until the eve of the wedding anniversary to his ex-wife.

As he wondered down past the various local businesses selling coffee, books, and nonsensical cure-alls using mystical methods, he happened upon a fortune teller.

45

He was skeptical to say the least.

She probably just tells people what they want to hear, he thought and turned around. He started back down the street towards a young musician who strummed away on his guitar playing a medley of cover songs people had probably heard far too often.

He stood in front of the young man and peered down on him like a father staring at a child who had done something wrong. The anger wasn't towards the musician but rather himself for never being inspired.

Jeremy tossed a few coins into the man's guitar case and shuffled slowly to a nearby bench. *What am I doing with my life?* he thought.

It was at that moment he turned his gaze away from the street fellow and back to the fortune teller's shop. A young woman, maybe twenty years old, walked out with a haggard old woman. The young woman hugged the older one and started shelling out dollar after dollar.

Is she really paying that charlatan? Jeremy thought as he leaned back into the bench and sighed.

He closed his eyes and pondered the scene around him while the musician changed genres from alternative to classical. It was at that moment the young woman from made her way over to the bench and set down next to Jeremy who gave a brief hello and went back to his thoughts.

Maybe she would know. I should just ask her, he

thought. *But what if she brushes me off?*

The woman stared at her phone, typing away like she was in a deep conversation with a boyfriend or someone she just reconnected with after a long hiatus.

Jeremy tapped her shoulder with a touch soft as a feather hitting the ground.

No response.

He tapped her shoulder again, this time harder like he was pressing a sticky keyboard key.

"Can I help you?" the woman barked as though Jeremy had interrupted the most important conversation of her life.

"I saw you down there at that fortune teller's buildi-"

"So? Who are you to judge where people spend their money?" She was clearly not in the mood to answer any questions.

"I was just wondering how good she is?"

"Who? Madam Serenity?"

Of course, it was Madam Serenity. Jeremy thought. *No Fortune teller can have a normal name like Jane or Mary.*

He snapped himself out of his thoughts. "Yes. Is she actually worth it?"

"Totally! She helps me with all my problems.

Whenever I go to her, it's like, poof. They just disappear." Her demeanor changed from drone to peppy as she twirled her hair with a new confidence. Her problems were going away before Jeremy's eyes.

"But have any of her predictions come true?" Jeremy asked bluntly. He wasn't amused by the silly antics with her voice.

"She gets stuff right like all the time. Just the other day she said I would get engaged and I totally did!" She showed off the rock on her finger. Jeremy would never be able to afford one like that.

What could it hurt, I guess? Jeremy thought. He stood up and brushed off his khakis as though there was dirt that accumulated on them.

"Thanks for your time, Miss," he said to the lady while giving a small shrug.

"No probs!" she squeaked back at him before going back to her phone.

Jeremy made his way back across the road amid the cool night air. He stared at the cloudless sky on his way down the street and pointed out of a few constellations. The moon hung particularly low in the sky but aligned perfectly with the street.

Knock. Jeremy waited in front of the door, but after a minute there was still no answer.

Knock. Knock. Finally, the door swung open with the small chime of the bell. Madam Serenity stood in the doorway with her ring coated fingers clutching it closely. She wore a pastel green bandana around her head with moons across it and her face was surprisingly devoid of wrinkles.

"Come in my dear boy." She motioned with her other hand and turned around. She walked back inside letting the door creak to a close behind her. Jeremy Followed.

Inside Jeremy was greeted by the sight of crystals, magpie bones, and the smell of incense burning on a nearby stand shaped like the base to a mighty oak tree.

Madam Serenity moved through the curtains that hung over the back room. "I haven't got all night, Dearie!" she called.

Jeremy wanted to go further inside but found himself stuck in place from the odd sights in the shop. He stared at a taxidermy cat placed on a small round table next to a red leather chair. Its piercing green eyes stared back at him, and despite it being stuffed, its black hair seemed to stand up like it was angry at him for entering its domain.

Jeremy's feet slid forward across the rickety wooden floor toward the back room, all the while not taking his gaze off the cat whose eyes seem to follow him. The touch of the curtains made him shake his head.

He stepped through to a shaded room, with a large round table covered by a red cloth. Pillows were placed on either side and black curtains with the same star signs he had seen outside graced the walls. A lone crystal ball was placed in the center of the table.

"Come, come, sit down," Madam Serenity said as she motioned to the pillow across from her. "This will only take a minute."

"Sorry," Jeremy said. He took his seat on the pillow, sitting cross-legged like they teach kids in kindergarten. "What am I supposed to do?"

"That depends, Dearie. What is it that you are looking for?"

"Inspiration mostly," Jeremy replied. "You see, I'm a writer, and I haven't been inspired in a long time. Most of my work is-"

"Enough," Madam Serenity said. "You want to be inspired. Inspiration doesn't come easily, no? Look in the crystal and tell me what you see."

Jeremy leaned himself forward and stared deeply into the crystal ball. Smoke filled the glass and swirl all around. Jeremy soon saw himself signing a book.

"That... That's me! I'm signing a book! Does this mean I actually write something good?" His eyes lit up with excitement. His jaw quivered from his nerves.

"You see. You will make it, Dearie."

"But how? I need to know what book will make me famous!"

"The price of such things is more than you want."

Jeremy whipped out his wallet. His last few twenties where nothing compared to what he could have. He tossed them out on the table like they were mere scraps of paper.

"Please, show me. I need to know."

"As you wish, Dearie," Madam Serenity said as she waved her ring covered hand over the crystal ball.

The smoke swirled once more, and Jeremy leaned in closer. The smoke cleared to reveal Jeremy holding a book titled, *"Murdering Anton."* It had a shaven, African fellow on the front with large glasses and X's over his eyes. His beard was short and styled well as if he took pride in grooming himself each morning.

"Hmm... I don't recognize that one."

"Perhaps you haven't started it, Dearie."

"I need to get writing this!" Jeremy jumped up from his pillow.

Madam Serenity pulled out a deck of tarot cards and began to shuffle. She spread the deck out across the table. "One for the road, Dearie? Could help reveal your passage."

Jeremy shrugged and took a card, and without looking at it, bolted out of the shop with a gleeful gleam across his face. He walked with an upbeat pace back down the street to catch the bus to get home.

The girl he had met earlier was still sitting on the bench. He gave a nod as he passed.

"How was it?" the girl called out. Jeremy had thought she wouldn't pay him any mind.

"Did she give you a tarot card?" the girl called out again.

Jeremy stopped to face her, but to his surprise, she was gone. He turned to the musician who was playing a soft acoustic melody to match the still night air.

"Did you see where she went?" Jeremy asked.

The musician shook his head. Jeremy pulled out the tarot card that Madam Serenity gave him.

The Hanged Man. He pondered on what that could mean for a minute before he noticed the bus pull up along the street. He ran down to it, barely making it to the door before it shut.

About an hour later he returned home, threw himself onto his couch with various stains from late night drinking ventures, and stared at the tarot card before setting it down on his coffee table amidst the bottles of hard liquor.

He pulled out his laptop and opened a blank document. The curser blinked as though it was taunting him to pour out his soul.

But nothing.

Nothing came out of his mind besides the titled which glared back at him begging to have a story written beneath it.

He downed the rest of a bottle of rum that was nearby before laying back and eventually falling asleep.

He awoke the next day with the normal headache that came from a lack of productivity and a stomach full of booze. He decided right away to go back down to Madam Serenity's storefront and confront her about his lack of inspiration.

He got ready, put on a long sleeve shirt and khakis, and rushed out the door without eating breakfast.

The street was busier than the previous night. Musicians lined the street corners all playing a different tune. Artists painted murals on the sides of buildings and shop owners welcomed people in with open arms. Jeremy didn't care about any of it. His mission was clear as he marched his was up the street past people calling out about their wares and preppy girls like the ones last night taking selfies.

Jeremy was so focused on his goal that he accidentally ran into a man, knocking him over. Jeremy apologized immediately and extended his arm to help the man up.

The man turned to face Jeremy and to his surprise, it was the man from the book cover.

"My bad, Anton," Jeremy blurted out.

Anton looked at Jeremy with one eyebrow raised in confusion. "How did you know my name?"

"Umm…" Jeremy's face was struck with concern.

He took a moment to look Anton over. Blue collared shirt that an I.T. guy might wear, khaki pants, and sandals that screamed it was his day off and he wanted to relax.

"Wait…" Anton paused for a moment with his hand under his chin and squinted eyes. "You're from the office Christmas party!" He snapped his fingers into a point that shocked Jeremy. "Brett, right?" Anton asked.

Jeremy gave a sharp breath, "Yup, that's me."

Anton patted Jeremy's shoulder. "I gotta get going, but it was good seein' you again."

Jeremy gave a sigh of relief as Anton continued past him up the street. It was in that moment that Jeremy had the idea. *I need to follow him.*

And that's what Jeremy did. For the rest of the day, he kept a distance from Anton while he followed him around town.

He got to know Anton a little bit better at each stop. There was the bookstore where Jeremy watched from behind an open book as Anton bought three horror novels and had a friendly chat with the girl behind the counter like they had been best friends from youth.

The second stop was the grocery store where Jeremy watched as Anton picked out a few vegetables: kale, bell peppers, zucchini, spaghetti squash. Nothing out of the ordinary for a man who like to eat healthy.

He followed Anton home to a bad part of town where cops generally stopped people to make sure they weren't up to anything and kids avoided playing in the streets.

Jeremy hid behind a dumpster as he watched the cops stop Anton. They pushed him around a bit which was typical for them. One checked Anton's bag while the other kept his right hand to his belt near where his gun was holstered. Standard behavior for cops in the area. Always thinking everything was dangerous.

When they let Anton go, Jeremy climbed up the fire escape, each step creaking as he walked which terrified him all the more with worry that he might get caught or the police would make him a suspect. Luckily for him, he was concealed in an alleyway shadowed by the setting sun.

It was on the fourth floor that he finally saw Anton enter one of the apartments. An older woman, perhaps forty, opened the door and through the muffled vibrations of the glass, Jeremy could hear something about needing to take the trash out.

Perhaps his mother, Jeremy though as he sat perched on the fire escape occasionally leaning into get a look at what Anton was doing. Nothing out of the ordinary. He played online with a few friends, did chores, read his book. Nothing about him said that he would be the victim of a terrible crime.

Jeremy peered into Anton's bedroom. The time on the glow-in-the-dark clock said 2:12AM, and Jeremy could hardly keep his eyes open anymore.

Time to go home. Jeremy got up to leave, but

something compelled him to take a picture of Anton with his phone before climbing back down the fire escape. The flash startled him, and he jumped backwards hitting the railing. The light flickered on, but before Anton could see who it was Jeremy was down the fire escape and back on the street.

Jeremy walked the streets with little fear that he might be mugged or arrested. He didn't stick out after all, and why would the cops want to come after some random white guy?

Maybe I'll take the bus, he thought, but the buses stopped running a few hours prior, so he was forced to use one of those rideshare companies people are always talking about.

He waited until he was out of the section of town worried that Anton might have followed him. It didn't take long to for the car to arrive, a sedan, something low-key. Jeremy hopped in, and the driver rounded the corner towards his home. The ride didn't take long for Jeremy. Instead of staring out the window at the street signs, bars, and businesses, he stared at the picture he had gotten of Anton sleeping away, curled up in plaid blankets and resting on an old-fashioned feather-stuffed pillow.

The sedan pulled up to Jeremy's home, and he went inside. He grabbed a bottle of rum from his table, laid back into the couch, and took a large swig.

Maybe tomorrow, Jeremy thought as he pulled out his phone to stare at the picture once more. He opened his laptop and began to write about the events that day, careful not to miss a single detail.

The sun rose at approximately 7AM, but Jeremy was up well before that nursing a headache. A printed picture of Anton now lay on his coffee table amidst the liquor bottles and wood stains.

Jeremy felt compelled to watch Anton, his mind fixated on knowing everything there could be about Anton's life, so he could retell it for his story. Jeremy rushed out the door around 7:30AM and reached the apartment at 8:15AM. He scaled the fire escape like an assassin, skulking each step of the way hoping nobody would catch him in the light.

He peered into Anton's room. *Still asleep,* Jeremy thought. He laid his back up against the brick well like last night with his legs bent and head resting on his knees. Children screamed from their porches at one another yelling out the occasional slang and curse that mothers would whoop them over the head about.

Jeremy stared at the grated walkway of the fire escape between his knees until he heard an alarm at 8:30AM. It rang out with one of those ear-piercing buzzes. Anton yawned and shuffled from his bed as Jeremy watched through the slightly faded curtains.

Anton's routine was almost scripted. Jeremy watched as Anton got up, took a shower behind a closed door, brushed his teeth, and got dressed all within ten minutes. It was well-timed, robotic. Jeremy followed across the fire escape as Anton sat down for breakfast as soon as his mother placed a plate down. Chicken and waffles, a favorite of Jeremy's was on the menu, and as his stomach growled like a bear waking from hibernation. He realized how hungry he was after skipping breakfast and dinner the night before.

Anton left the apartment at 8:50AM. Jeremy crept his way down the fire escape and watched every movement. Anton walked down the street towards Jeremy, but Jeremy hid behind a trashcan before anyone could notice.

The day wasn't extremely interesting. Anton walked to work and arrived at the normal time of 9:00AM, to which his boss complained that he was late even though work started at that exact time. Jeremy posted himself in a few places; the coffee shop across the street, the bench out front, even leaned against the wall near the window where he could turn his head to get a glance at Anton as he filed papers and took phone calls throughout the day.

Jeremy watched him for a little while before wandering off to find some food at a local diner where he ordered the chicken and waffles same as Anton.

After a long day's work, Anton marched out of the office with a smirk and bright eyes while tossing an apple like he was some sort of bigshot. He went down to the bus stop and stood among other well-dressed gentlemen all wearing coats and ties.

Jeremy sat across the street on a bench staring at his phone, trying to get a good picture in between passing cars. He snapped a good one with Anton's apple in the air just before he missed it and it bounced off the ground. Anton bent forward to pick it up off the street as the bus pulled in quickly off the bus road. Jeremy sat up, eyes wide, like he was finally going to witness what would bring him great inspiration. He had a front row seat to the tragedy.

The bus horn blared. Anton jumped and a loud thud rang out.

But nothing. Anton had moved just in time to avoid the bus's front-end colliding with his skull. A passerby struck the side to get the driver to open the door as if nothing happened.

Jeremy sat back in the bench, defeated. He kicked the bench with his heel, knowing he should give up, but he just couldn't.

He decided to go home after the poor events of the day and fixed himself what he thought Anton might be having for dinner: tacos. It was Taco Tuesday, after all, and a mixture of spices helped the flavor and the heat.

He compiled a list of all the events of the day; each time Anton was questioned by his boss, each bathroom trip, and yes, even a list of each snack that he watched Anton take from his desk. Jeremy added his own writer's flair to it though to make everything seem better than it actually was and laid back into the couch.

As Jeremy stared up at his ceiling with the seven-o-clock sun still partially in the sky, he felt the need to go back to Anton's apartment, but resisted the urge knowing that it would be another boring night. He drifted off into a much-needed sleep, but even that gave him urges he couldn't explain.

On a normal night, Jeremy couldn't ever recall dreaming. It was something he lacked as a person. He used to listen to ex-girlfriends' dreams and think that they were lucky to be able to let their minds wander into blissful imagery.

Tonight, was different.

Instead of the black void that filled Jeremy's mind, Anton was there. Jeremy watched as Anton went about his normal routine, but when it came to the end of the day, Jeremy pictured Anton dying. He was struck by a bullet and Jeremy ran to his aid and clutched him close. Jeremy applied pressure to the wound, but blood continued to pour out.

He ripped his hands away and reached for a towel, but when he turned back, the hole in Anton's chest stopped bleeding and started leaking pennies, dimes, you name it. Cash flowed out on to the road. Jeremy hugged Anton's corpse and kissed its forehead again and again.

"You've made me rich," he exclaimed.

Jeremy woke up and checked his hands for signs of blood along with the floor around him for signs of money, nothing. It was 7:00AM, and he was ready to start his day. He chronicled his dream in case it had semblance in the story he would write and rushed out to Anton's with a skip in his step.

Like before, he perched himself on Anton's apartment's fire escape, ready to catch the morning routine. This time was different. Jeremy felt the urge to walk into the room, to catch Anton off-guard, to do the job himself.

That will never work! He yelled at his own thoughts. Angry for thinking he could manifest his own destiny. *This isn't a novel*, he thought. *Things don't work that way.*

He remained calm and watched Anton as he hit every beat of the morning routine right on schedule. There was something interesting about watching someone who was quite different than Jeremy. Jeremy spent his life jumping from one thing to the next, always leaving a trail wherever he went, desperate to one day make it in the world. Anton had everything mapped out and it became more apparent the more Jeremy watched his movements.

Days turned to weeks and Jeremy began to notice things, like how Anton brought his mother fresh flowers each time the old ones died because she never watered them. He flashed a smile and took deep breaths whenever the flowers caught his eye.

Jeremy also learned a lot about Anton's life, like how is mother and father split up and his little brother and sister stayed with his father. His sister was young, maybe seven or eight, and loved ballet. Anton walked her to ballet practice every Saturday when his mother told him to at exactly 9:00AM and have her there no later than 9:15AM.

Anton would also take his brother, who was about thirteen or fourteen, to karate practice each Saturday afternoon once ballet let out. His brother wasn't the same as Anton and their sister. The two of them were very timely and well-managed, while their brother threw fits about doing the simplest things. He was the type to get mixed up in just about anything that would make him money since he would sneak out during class to meet with his crummy looking friends. It was obvious that he got involved with karate as a way to bring structure to his life.

Each act that Jeremy witnessed brought him closer in his mind to Anton. It was like he was sharing a life with him from the outside of a window, forever looking in. As the days progressed and quickly turned to weeks, it became clear to Jeremy this was about more than just riches. There was a connection there Jeremy couldn't explain, and as much as he wanted Anton to die and fulfill his fantasies, part of him wanted to keep Anton around.

Jeremy continued to catalogue the events of the day each night, upgrading to a tablet so he could write at night while sleeping on Anton's apartment's fire escape. It was as close as he was willing to get without breaking the boundaries and revealing his presence.

One important Saturday came about. It was early in the morning about two weeks into watching Anton. It started off normal, the normal routine, breakfast, and then marching over to his father's house to walk his little sister to ballet. She was nervous to go back to class after being bullied and her hesitant hand grasped Anton's as she shook her head each time he tried to open the door. She was stubborn, just like her mother.

It was then that Jeremy saw a new side of Anton as he watched from the other side of the road leaning next to a broken down and forgotten phone booth. He watched as Anton dragged her little sister inside and brought her to the dressing room. The other little girls looked like they were doing their normal point and laugh routine, but that all stopped when the both of them emerged from the room dressed in black spandex. Form fitting and leaving much nothing to the imagination.

Jeremy couldn't help but be amazed by the sight. His feelings were conflicted, angry that he wanted to get a closer look. It was in that moment as he inched himself closer to the street, that he realized there was something more at play than wanting Anton to die. He had felt a connection to Anton, one he hadn't had for a long time.

Jeremy soon started staring from in front of the window as Anton twirled with his little sister, leapt, and even attempted a split. It was all to make his little sister feel more included among the other girls. Soon a large crowd formed, all chuckling and taking videos of the guy in spandex leaping across a room.

Jeremy wandered out of the crowd and sat on a bench nearby. Anton stepped out, back in his normal paper-pushing attire. Jeremy gazed over at him and wanted nothing more than to confront Anton and commend him for being brave enough to help his sister out in that way. His foot moved over, begging Jeremy to take that first step, but he couldn't.

He wouldn't.

He refused to give himself away out of fear that Anton would reject him. If he accidentally exposed too much, his plan would be ruined. So, he sat there, buried his head in a newspaper someone had left and softly wept out of desperation.

Sully with guilt, Jeremy returned home instead of watching his victim. He laid down on his couch and stared up the first picture of Anton that he kept nearby.

I must get it together, he thought. *I need to remember. He must die, so that I may finally get the inspiration I need. I can't forget that.*

And that's how it went. Jeremy shoved his feelings aside deep in that vault we all carry inside ourselves and took a break from seeing Anton.

Agony.

It was agony staying away, but Jeremy knew he had to get his head in the right place. He drew pictures of Anton that he hung all over his walls and each time he hung a new one, he etched out the eyes so they wouldn't stare back at him.

The week dragged on yet no number of pictures on the walls could ever stop Jeremy from having feelings for his victim, but it was a start. He trusted himself to go back out on his hunt. He packed all his belongings and trekked out into the night air.

Jeremy twitched as he walked down the roads to Anton's apartment. He turned back a few times just to double back around. He reached Anton's apartment at 11:30PM. Anton should have been sleeping. The street was quiet; no cops, no cars, no children with parents yelling at them to come in. Just the occasional passerby with what looked like ill intent.

Jeremy scaled the fire escape like he used to. Quick, determined, ready to watch Anton through the night. He peered into Anton's room. Nothing, just a well-made bed, perfectly tucked and maintained. He checked Anton's mother's room. Sound asleep.

Jeremy wanted to knock on the door and ask where Anton was, but his mother probably didn't know. It was Saturday, karate day.

Jeremy walked off, cloaked in the darkness of the street, the clouds helping to hide him as he skulked down the road in his black suede jacket and blackened pants. No streetlights, no moon, just himself and his thoughts.

What am I doing? I should have turned back.

But what if he needs me?

He doesn't need me.

But what if he is going to die. I must be there.

Stop with this stupid fetish.

Keep going.

He trudged onward, lost in his mixed-up madness. He reached the karate studio. Empty. No lights, no music, no kids screaming as they punched and kicked.

Silence.

Jeremy took out the tarot card he received so long ago and stared at the image of the man hanging from the tree.

Anton must die for me to gain fortune.

He needs to suffer.

He needs to be set free.

Crash! The loud slam of a metal door rang from across the street. Jeremy jumped but saw no one.

He crept across the road. People were talking in harsh tones. The loud voices escalated to yelling. Jeremy sat beside the door. He could hear Anton's brother but couldn't make out the words. He pressed his ear quietly against the door, but muffled words rang back.

"Don't shoot!" Anton cried out.

Jeremy could hear it plain as day. A sinister smile glared across his face. He inched the door open as to not make a single sound that would catch the shooters off guard.

It was a warehouse, filled with crates, plenty of places to hide. He chose a spot that was easy to see. Two armed men, both pasty like fresh cream. Suave looking guys wearing flashy watches and fine suits who were quick to anger. It seemed like Anton's brother had finally crossed into the wrong territory.

Anton and his brother had their hands up, defenseless. All Jeremy could do was stare in amazement; laptop close so he could chronicle it all later.

"Give us the money," one of the pasty men demanded.

Anton motioned to his brother who shrugged.

"I don't got anything," he responded.

Anton looked angry. The first time Jeremy had ever seen his eyebrows furled. He couldn't help but admire it. Strict, yet protective.

"I'm going to slowly reach for the money," Anton said as he reached down into his pocket and pulled out his wallet. He tossed it over to the two men. "Should be three hundred in there. Will that be enough?"

One of the men grabbed the wallet, keeping his gun trained on Anton and his brother. He set the gun on a crate and counted the money.

"It's all here," the man said.

Jeremy clenched his jaw and gritted his teeth. His eyes began to grow fierce. *You've got to be kidding me.*

The two men walked out of the warehouse, chatting it up as they went. The door creaked open and closed with a bang that echoed through the warehouse.

"Man, if you hadn't stepped in, I could've handled it," Anton's brother blurted out.

Anton sighed. "You doing all this illegal shit is what made me get dragged in in the first place! Why don't you ever listen to me? I just had to give up my paycheck to help you get out of a jam!"

Anton's brother grew quiet. Jeremy's rage

continued to grow, hidden behind the crate.

"I didn't need you!" Anton's brother cried.

"If I wasn't here, then you'd be dead already!"

Must I do everything myself!

Jeremy stood up from behind the crate in view of the bothers, but they paid him no mind in their squabble. He cleared his throat loud enough to make his presence known, and the brothers stopped to stare at the man in black who had no business being there.

Jeremy stood as a hot mess, his hair in shambles, outfit crooked, and smile on his face that screamed murder.

"You've got to be kidding me!"

Anton and his brother stepped back.

"I spent weeks! Weeks! And now... Nothing!" Jeremy began to drool slightly, his scraggly beard catching it. "Do you know the toll it took on me?"

Anton stepped forward. "I don't know what this is, but it'll be okay buddy."

Jeremy swung his arm up. "Typical, Anton. Always trying to play the bigger man. Always trying to do good! This was supposed to be perfect!"

"Do you need help old man?" Anton's brother blurted out.

Jeremy turned his gaze to match the brother's.

"You! You just couldn't get this to end another way!"

Anton looked over to his brother. "Go get help," he said calmly. The look on his eyes screamed danger.

Jeremy noticed the gun left behind by the men. Anton's brother ran as Jeremy picked it up and fired. Bang! The bullet rang out and echoed through the warehouse catching into one of the steel support beams.

Anton cowered before the madman with the gun.

"You couldn't have just gotten killed! You had to be the safe guy! The guy nobody cares about!"

"What are you talking about?" Anton asked with tears welling in his eyes.

"I waited for weeks! Hoping for God knows what to happen, but boring Anton didn't so much as get a scratch!" Jeremy began flailing the gun around like it was a toy and he was a kid on a playground. He soon found himself next to the wall of the warehouse.

"Did you know I fell for you? I thought, maybe it wouldn't be so bad. Maybe we could have a fling. Maybe you didn't have to die. Talked myself out of that though."

"Maybe if you put down the gun, we can talk this out. No need for violence." Anton tried conveying the message through his hands, but Jeremy was too far gone.

Kill him, Jeremy's thoughts screamed.

"No, I can't. He needs to die naturally!"

"I don't need to die," Anton cried. "We can work this out. We can get you help."

The sounds of sirens rang out in the distance. Jeremy clutched his head to try and quell the voices.

Kill him!

"No!"

Do it!

"No!" he screamed. He slammed his gun toting hand into the wall of the warehouse.

It all happened in slow motion for Jeremy. The gun went off. The bullet flew through the air and struck one of the supports. It ricocheted off and struck Anton in the neck. Blood flowed out across his fresh white polo shirt.

The gun dropped to the floor. Jeremy ran over to catch Anton as he fell. Anton landed in Jeremy's lap. The hanged man tarot card dropped to the floor from Jeremy's pocket.

"Why?" Anton gurgled. Blood dripped from his cool lips.

"I don't know... I didn't want it to be this way."

"You didn't need to..."

Anton's body fell limp. Jeremy's eyes swelled with tears, one dripping onto Anton's forehead. He kissed his lips in an attempt to breathe new life into him, but nothing. Nothing could save Anton now.

Jeremy reached for the tarot card laying in a pool of blood. He placed it on Anton's chest.

Bang! Another shot rang out in the room. The sound of flesh ripping followed. Jeremy looked down at the hole in his chest. Blood streamed down his dirty shirt.

The trails of blood that streamed from the two men blended. Their fates intertwined. Anton's brother held his hands in the air as the cops swarmed the building.

The police collected everything of Jeremy's. They read his tale of twisted romance which led to the shooting.

Anton's brother was let go. The police branded him a hero for killing a madman. He never felt the same after that night.

He took to writing, jotted down every action that took place in the night. Years later, Anton's brother was traveling the nation for his new book, "*Murdering Anton.*" On the cover sat Jeremy, clenching onto Anton. Above Jeremy's head was the card.

The hanged man.

Caged

Ivy chokes as the stiff air fills her lungs. The residue of mildew tickles her throat. She coughs, and metal clanks with each convulsion. Blood drips from her wrists and a faint stream of light crosses over her. She glances down at her hand which is shackled to a three-foot cubic metal cage. Ivy whimpers, as the shackles cut her skin. Her throat is dry; her cough echoes in the room.

The stream of light increases as the night grows darker. Ivy peers through the steel bars of her prison and follows the light. She glances upon a rectangular window far across the room. Through it, a sliver of the full moon plays peekaboo with Ivy. She appreciates the light, but at the same time, wishes it would go away. In the dark, it is easy to deal with the fact that she is a dirty bloody mess. In the light, it's hard for Ivy to escape from reality. Most days, which she failed to track since month three, she slips away into an alternate reality and dreams about how different things could have gone if she just stayed home. Ivy loved going to the fair, but this year was the year everything changed.

***

Over the summer Ivy's best friend Cam moved away. She always talked about moving with her, but the reality was, she was too scared. They did everything together, and when the fair came to town, Ivy couldn't bare going with anyone else. She had her work friends, but she didn't really know them. One day after work, her coworker John mustered up the courage to talk to her. He was attracted to her loneliness and the fantasy of saving Ivy from her misery.

"Hey, me and a couple of friends are going to the fair, if you want to tag along," said John.

Ivy was sitting at the break room table staring off into space. Her eyes adjusted to meet his.

"I don't know, I think I'd rather stay home," she said.

John sat across from her, and trying to convince her to come, "Oh, c'mon it'll be fun, I promise. It's better than sitting around staring at the wall."

"I like staring at the wall. It gives me room to daydream on a blank surface."

"What are you daydreaming about?" John asked.

"None of your business," Ivy replied. She was

dreaming about another co-worker, Colin.

"Fair enough. Well, if you change your mind, here's my number." John slid a piece of paper across the table and left it just above Ivy's hands. "I hear they have a legit psychic. Maybe she can predict some happiness for you," John said as he left the room.

Ivy rolled her eyes. She never believed in superstition. So, she went home and continued to daydream while she laid on her soft mattress, staring at the ceiling, her blank canvas to conjure up a new life and a better version of her reality. She couldn't stop thinking about what John said. Maybe it seemed silly to virtually experience life. After all, she will eventually run out of experiences to reminisce. She slowly got ready as she looked over the piece of paper with John's number. Her heart sped up at the thought of calling him.

"This is so stupid," Ivy muttered to herself. "Screw it." She dialed John's number and pressed the speakerphone.

"Ivy! You changed your mind."

"Yeah, I guess."

"Great! Come to Madame Oracle at the center of the fair."

Ivy walked through the fair searching for this so-called psychic.

"Oh, hell no," she said.

A bright flashing sign read 'Psychic on Duty' on a

metal caravan. A sticker on the door read 'Best psychic this side of the Mediterranean.'

"What does that even mean?" Ivy questioned.

The metal door creaked open, and Ivy entered the heavily adorned caravan. There were gold silk hangings and talisman strung throughout the room. Velvet sheets were strewn across the floor, and she felt she was walking as royalty. Ivy chuckled, as her disbelief grew.

"So tacky," Ivy whispered to herself.

"Come in. Come in my dear," an old woman said.

Ivy crossed through the door frame hangings to the back of the caravan. An old woman dressed in the usual psychic garb stood before her. She was adorned in gold jewelry and even wore an Oracle hat. A crystal ball drew Ivy's attention to the table where she sat.

"So, how does this work? I tell you a little about myself, and you come up with some generic life lessons?" Ivy said.

"Don't be so quick to judge, my dear," said Madame Oracle. "You might be surprised at what you hear. Now, keep quiet, and head my warning. Your energy is like fire. I could feel it before you entered."

"Warning?"

Madame Oracle places a deck of tarot cards on the table.

"Take your pick," she said to Ivy.

Ivy picked her cards and Madame Oracle placed them on the table. She shuddered at what the cards revealed. Her hand shook as her long fingernail pointed to the justice card as it was paired with the death card.

"You must leave this place. You were better off at home with your fantasies."

"Why? This is total garbage. Let me see that deck."

Madame Oracle swiped the cards off of the table, her eyes glazed over, and her body convulsed. "No, no! You must leave now or suffer a solitary life confined in someone else's sick fantasy. Except, this fantasy is very real, my dear. Heed this warning or find yourself trapped as many others have been before you. Trust no one. This is your only chance, now get out!"

"What? I'm not paying for you to yell at me," said Ivy.

Madame Oracle bangs on the table and leans forward meeting Ivy's face, "Money is no concern for me. You must leave now."

"Sure thing. Best psychic, my rear end."

Ivy left the caravan and walked around the festival. She spotted John through a crowd. He was with her crush, Colin. Ivy waved her arm fiercely in the air, as she jumped up high hoping he would see her. This was her chance to impress her crush and hang out with John.

"John, over here!"

John caught himself as he turned to the call of his

name.

"John! It's Ivy; look behind you."

Ivy waved and ran in John's direction. She had a smile on her face, like a happy go lucky dog who found its' owner. She passed through a crowd near a lighted festival ride, but Ivy's body acted on its own as it pulled to the side. Her eyes fixated on a peculiar yellow van parked along the festival gates before she was forced to an alleyway. Her mouth was covered by a large, sweaty hand. The taste of metal touched her taste buds, as the dirty ring of the hand rubbed against her lips. Ivy's screams were muffled and drowned out by the happy screams of the rollercoaster ride. A tear trickled down Ivy's cheek as she recalled the warning she so blatantly ignored by Madame Oracle.

***

The dark room where Ivy is held, loses the light of the moon. Her dreams fade as reality sinks in.

"This is what I get for trying to 'make connections.' Thanks for nothing, Cam," Ivy mutters to herself.

The floorboard creaks as Ivy falls deep into her fantasy of what could have been. She looks up, but no one is there.

"Hello?" she yells. "Anyone there, asshole?"

A light above Ivy's cage flickers. Ivy squints as the fluorescent light kisses her face. She is mesmerized by the brightness this night, of all nights, has given her. She is lost in the illumination before the presence of a blood-soaked figure, pierced with knives, flashes before her. Ivy gasps and retreats to the back corner of her cage. Her chains clatter and echo through the room just before the light bulb bursts. The glass shatters all around her and grazes her cheek. She touches the wound and looks at the blood.

"What was that?" she asks herself. "It's fine. I'm fine. Dehydration, that's it. Dehydration leads to hallucinations just like a mirage in a desert." Ivy scurries to the corner of her cage where she has etched tallies for each passing day.

"Five, ten, fifteen, twenty, twenty-five," Ivy continued to count her tallies to understand how long she has been missing from the world.

"They are looking for me." Ivy nods her head in agreement with herself. "It's normal, police procedure, and John, well he is obsessed with me. He must be looking for me." "Ivy's eyes swell with tears. Her lips tremble as she fully recognizes her devastation. The mere thought of being forgotten is unacceptable to Ivy, even though ten, twenty, thirty days have passed her by without rescue.

Each day begins with a pile of slop inches away from her cage. A spoon is conveniently placed at arm's length. If she eats, a bucket waits for her to defecate into. The smell is what she can only imagine death is like. Little does she notice the beading eyes watching her as she adapts to her new life. Every night the figure with one-hundred knives stands over Ivy as she sleeps. It studies her, even pulls out a knife from its own rotted flesh to caress her while it fantasizes about a new partner to spend its life with.

Ivy rustles around as the cold steel touches her cheek. Her eyes open to the blurry presence before her. She jolts awake and cowers to the edge of her cage. Her chest tightens, and her heart races.

The stabbed figure scrapes its knife across the metal cage. Ivy covers her ears to the high-pitched scraping. The figure appears right in front of Ivy. Its tattered flesh drips with blood. Skin appears to melt right off of its so-called face. One thing Ivy knows for sure, is it is staring into the window of her soul. She whimpers with fright as the thing examines her fear.

It opens its mouth, and a low raspy voice says, "Will you be my friend?" It stares into her eyes and forces a crooked smile like mechanical levers are pulling at its smile muscles. Ivy screams and closes her eyes.

"It's only a nightmare., I am still asleep," she says confidently. Ivy opens her eyes with caution.

Inches away from Ivy is the figure's face.

"Boo! You can't escape hell, dear," the figure says.

"What do you mean?" asks Ivy. Ever since she ended up in the cage she dreams of her escape.

She imagines her savior would be Colin from work. Her mind trails back to the carnival. Colin catches a glimpse of Ivy's legs dragging along the ground. He rushes to her aid, and punches the man who nearly kidnapped her. John interjects himself in her fantasy. She shakes her head. It only made sense that a love taken away before its blossom could only get redemption.

The figure looks around the dark room. "I was like you, girl," the figure says. "I had dreams, a family, a plan to kill the fucker who kidnapped me."

It snaps back to focus on Ivy and sits next her.

"But let me let you in on a little something…"

It gently grabs Ivy by the cheeks.

"You're gonna die here!"

The stabbed figure disappears, and Ivy grabs her cheeks to feel the cold impression the figure left. She looks around where the knife scraped along the bottom of her cage. Writing appears to be etched into the metal. It reads: *Micah. 23. One year.*

Ivy presses her fingertips along the etching. "One year?" she questions. She falls deep into her fantasy of what could have been if she wasn't so interested in meeting John.

"Stupid, stupid fucking girl. If you weren't so focused on. I don't know…, dating, then you wouldn't have been captured, ya dumb fuck.

A door slams followed by heavy footsteps. A tall figure wearing a suit, flips a light switch, but the lights fail to turn on.

"I've been watching you," he says. "Sand you know what I think? I don't care for your attitude, your will to live."

The man raises a knife to Ivy. The glint of moonlight shines on the man. "Colin?" Ivy asks.

Instead of the knife impaling her, it sinks deep into Colin's chest.

Ivy, confused and in disbelief, calls out, "Micah?"

"Even though I lived every day in hell, doesn't mean someone else needs to."

Ivy's cage unlocks, and she bolts to the exit door. The sun peeks over the horizon and warms her skin. She runs to the street, but for a moment looks back at the building she was held captive for thirty some odd days.

"I will make sure they know who you are, Micah."

ABOUT THE AUTHORS

Joan McHugh

Joan McHugh is an author and screenwriter. Her journey to become a creative writer started at a young age when her teacher would put daily writing prompts on the projector. Her imagination grew as she attended Full Sail University and graduated with honors receiving a Bachelor's Degree in Creative Writing for Entertainment. Afterward, she was published by Scarlet Leaf Review and Horror Addicts for her flash fiction stories. When she is not creating the fictional downfall of a beloved character, she enjoys spending time with her daughter.

Aden Carter

Aden Carter started his writing career by creating quests for tabletop games. His stories led to him pursuing a Bachelor's Degree in Creative Writing from Full Sail University. Carter currently writes articles for gaming websites and spends his free time at the table guiding adventurers through quests for glory. He hopes to one day create a story that is beloved by many, not for money, but to leave his mark on the world.